Ronnie's Treasure Hunt

Written by **Pippa Goodhart**
Illustrated by Deborah Allwright

A & C Black • London

For my nephew
David Goodheart, with love

FIFE COUNCIL	
043158	
PETERS	19-Nov-2012
JF	£4.99
JICR	KY

Reprinted 2011
First paperback edition 2007
First published 2006 by
A & C Black Publishers Ltd
36 Soho Square, London,W1D 3QY

www.acblack.com

Text copyright © 2006 Pippa Goodhart
Illustrations copyright © 2006 Deborah Allwright

The rights of Pippa Goodhart and Deborah Allwright to be identified as the
author and illustrator of this work respectively has been asserted by them
in accordance with the Copyrights, Designs and Patents Act 1988.

ISBN 978-0-7136-7596-2

A CIP catalogue for this book is available from the British Library.

This book is produced using paper that is made from wood grown in
managed, sustainable forests. It is natural, renewable and recyclable.
The logging and manufacturing processes conform to the
environmental regulations of the country of origin.

Printed and bound in Singapore by Tien Wah Press (Pte) Ltd

Chapter One

"I'm bored," said Ronnie. He kicked the table and a box of biscuits fell onto the floor.

"Now look what you've done!" said his mum. "Here's me trying to tidy up and there's you making more mess!"
"Sorry," said Ronnie.
"And I'm a mess, too," said his mum, sadly.

"Everything's a mess!"
"Don't worry," said Ronnie. "It's your
birthday tomorrow. That'll cheer you up."
But he hadn't bought her a present yet.
What could he get to make her happy?

Ronnie looked in his piggy bank.
It was empty.

He looked in his pockets and found one sticky, old sweet.

Well, thought Ronnie, since I don't have the money to buy a present, I'll just have to find one instead.

So he set off down the road, looking for things. He saw some flowers, but they weren't pretty. They were weeds.

He saw something shining, but it wasn't jewels or gold. It was a puddle.

Then he saw a rocket parked by the side
of the road.
"Wow!" said Ronnie. "Who's is that?"

"IT'S OURS! HA HAAA!"

Chapter Two

"Pirates!" said Ronnie. "What are you
doing in my road?"

"We're looking for treasure. Ha haaa!"
"Well, there isn't any treasure here,"
said Ronnie. "I've already looked."
"Ah, but we ain't hunting for treasure
down here," said the captain. "We're
hunting for treasure from the skies!"

Ronnie looked up at the cloudy sky.
"What treasure? There's no treasure
up there," he said.

"It's *hidden* treasure, boy! Hidden until night, when they put it on show. Have you never looked out of a night-time window and seen treasure sparkling in the sky?"

"No," said Ronnie.

"What, never seen that fat, round opal they calls the Moon?" roared the captain. "Never seen those diamonds up there, scattered in the sky?"

"Those aren't diamonds," said Ronnie. "They're stars."

"Call 'em what you like," said the captain. "I intend to have them twinklers just as soon as we've got ourselves a cabin boy for our spaceship rocket. Grab the boy, Dolly! Bind him up, Shanks!"

"But my mum…"

Shanks gagged Ronnie before he could
finish what he was saying. Then the
pirates pushed him into the rocket and
shut the door.

"Mmph bmph wmph!" mumbled
Ronnie.

"Shut up, boy, we're off
into space!"

19

"Countdown!" ordered the captain. "Ten – Nine – Seven – Two – Three – Lift off!" Nothing happened.
"What's wrong with this blooming rocket?" roared the captain.

"Untie the boy and let's hear what he
has to say!" said the captain.
"You've counted wrong," said Ronnie.
"It should go:

Chapter Three

They shot through the clouds and up into the clear sky above. Then it all went silent. There was nothing twinkling in space that Ronnie could see. Only the Sun blazing orange fire.

"We're not going to try and catch the Sun, are we?" asked Ronnie.

"Course not!" said the captain. "We're not stupid. That old Sun's too hot to touch. No, we're only after twinklers we can handle. And we must be ready to grab them quick when it all goes dark. Mr Shanks, get out the grabber and polish her up. Boy, you can mend the hole in the booty bag."

They all got busy, and soon it grew dark outside. Space was spotted with stars and planets.

The captain rubbed his hands together. "See? Lots and lots of lovely treasure!"

"That's the best one!" said Shanks,
pointing towards the biggest, shiniest star.
"It's only a rock with the sun shining
on it," said Ronnie.
But nobody took any notice of him.

"Steer Moon-starboard, Mr Shanks,"
ordered the captain. He held up a finger.
"See that twinkler? It'll fit nice in a ring."
The nearer they got to the twinkler,
the bigger and bigger it grew.

"What a whopper!" said the captain.
"Dolly, cook up something to give us
strength for grabbing. Boy, you can peel
the parsnips."

Dolly put sausages and parsnips and peas and potatoes into a pot. Then she threw in a pair of socks.

"What are you doing?" asked Ronnie.

"I'm washing the captain's socks," said Dolly. "No point in wasting hot water. Don't worry. I'll take them out before I serve up."

The pong from the pot was terrible.
"I ain't eating that!"
"You are!"
"I ain't!"

The pirates were so busy arguing that
they didn't notice they'd reached the
big twinkler until they hit it…

Chapter Four

"Everybody out!" said the captain.
"Bring the grabber and the booty bag!"
He opened the door and they all
climbed out.
Then they stopped still.

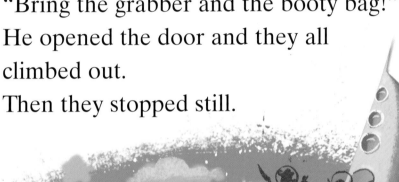

They were standing on dark, dusty rocks.
Nothing was twinkling.
"Oh," said the captain.
"Er," said Shanks.
"Um," said Dolly.

"I told you it wasn't a real diamond,"
said Ronnie.
But the captain was pointing at something.
"W-w-what's that?" he stammered.

"Just a little alien," said Ronnie.
"Help!" roared the captain. "It'll eat us
alive! Get back to the rocket. Quick!"
Shanks, Dolly and the captain ran…

But Ronnie was watching the alien.
It was sucking up dust and rocks, and
it was smiling. That's a strange diet,
thought Ronnie.

Ronnie bent down and stroked the alien.
It was soft. "Hello," he said.
"Burble blip," said the alien, then it
rested its head on Ronnie's lap and
looked up at him.
"I like you!" said Ronnie.

"And my mum would like you, too.
You could help clean up our messy house.
Would you like to come home with me?"
"Bloodle bess!" said the alien, and it
wagged all of its tails.

So Ronnie popped the alien into the booty bag and climbed back into the rocket. The engines roared and they began the countdown:

There was a great rush of rocket noise and they swooped into space.

Chapter Five

Ronnie saw Earth getting bigger. It was blue and green and white and beautiful.

He let the alien peep out of the bag to see. "That's where we're going," Ronnie whispered. "That's home."
"Zing ping!" said the alien.

"What did you say, boy?" asked the captain.

"Er, I said, perhaps we should sing," said Ronnie, stuffing the alien back into the bag.

"Sing?" said the captain.

"Yes, sing Happy Birthday to my mum," said Ronnie. "Today's her birthday. And you're all invited to my house for a party."
"I like parties!" said Shanks.
"We'll need to bring a present," said Dolly.

"I've got Mum's present here," said
Ronnie.
"What…?" began the captain. But he
didn't have time to say any more
because…

…they landed, back in Ronnie's road.

"Cor, look at that!" said Shanks as they climbed out of the rocket.
Everything on Earth was beautiful in the moonlight. Even the weeds looked pretty, so Ronnie picked some.

And when Ronnie's mum opened the door and stepped outside, she looked lovely, too. "Ronnie! Where on Earth have you been?" she said.

"I haven't been on Earth," said Ronnie.

"I've been in space! And I've brought you some presents. Look!"
Ronnie held out the flowers, and then he pulled the little alien from the bag.
"How lovely! Just what I need," said Ronnie's mum.

But Ronnie's mum was looking at the
captain. And he was gazing back at her.

"Would you see that!" said the captain.
"Just look at your mum's eyes, Ronnie.
I reckon I've found my twinklers after all."
So everyone was happy.